THE PECULIAR PLIGHT OF MILICENT WRYGHT

JOANNE DE SIMONE

ILLUSTRATED BY ANNETTE LEE

Castle Garden

Renton, Washington

Edited by S. C. Moore and C. E. Moore.
Cover Art and illustrations by Annette Lee.

Published 2016, Castle Garden Publications,
an imprint of Gazebo Gardens Publishing, LLC.
www.GazeboGardensPublishing.com

978-1-938281-67-9 (hardcover)
978-1-938281-68-6 (paperback)
978-1-938281-69-3 (e-book)

Library of Congress Control Number: 2015941217

Printed in the United States of America.

For my brother, Joseph.

Milicent Wryght, Manhattan socialite,
once lived on the Upper East Side.
Though she owned a world of material wealth,
she was unhappy deep down inside.
Neither laughed, nor cried from wounded pride,
and then one unfortunate day
she died.

Milicent Wryght, melancholy socialite,
went to her unhappy end,
quite suddenly and all alone,
and expired without one single friend.
With ruthless deeds no man could defend,
she perished with no time her ways to amend.

Milicent Wryght, Manhattan socialite,
was once lovely, all smiles and good cheer.
She met and married the man of her dreams,
but romance lasted less than a year.
Undone by foolish jealousy and fear,
her woeful tale will now be told here.

Milicent Wryght, Manhattan socialite,
had been married, and happily so.
She loved, laughed, dreamed, and danced,
with her kind, handsome, sensitive beau.
But all their serenity in an instant did go,
when her nature changed from dove to crow.

Milicent Wryght, malevolent socialite,
had a short time of wedded bliss.
Hubby's hobby was training homing pigeons,
and it was clear she bore prejudice.
Every pigeon became her arch nemesis,
and she vengefully vowed to put a stop to this.

Milicent Wryght, Manhattan socialite,
was jealous of the pigeons in flight.
Jealous when they roosted on the roof,
jealous when they slept at night.
Jealous when they huddled together tight.
Even jealous when the birds were out of sight.

Milicent Wryght, intolerant socialite,
grew so envious of his feathered friends,
'cause they took his time away from her,
leaving her alone for hours on end.
Her mate with them too much time did spend,
and at her protests, the birds he'd defend.

Milicent Wryght, begrudging socialite,
could not fathom her hubby's bliss.
While he cared for and nurtured dozens of birds,
she was aghast when he gave one a kiss.
She admonished him about being remiss,
"Well, it's me or them," she scornfully hissed.

Milicent Wryght, Manhattan socialite,
saw her husband was taken aback,
at his bride's envy of his placid pets—
said, "Mili, it's compassion you lack!"
She turned on him, beastly, like a maniac,
set her hand on his face with an angry
SMACK!

Milicent Wryght, brazen socialite,
quickly sensed her mistake in this.
Violence would not be condoned by him—
she offered a remorseful kiss.
Her hubby only saw her a stranger, an antagonist,
the meanest woman in all the metropolis.

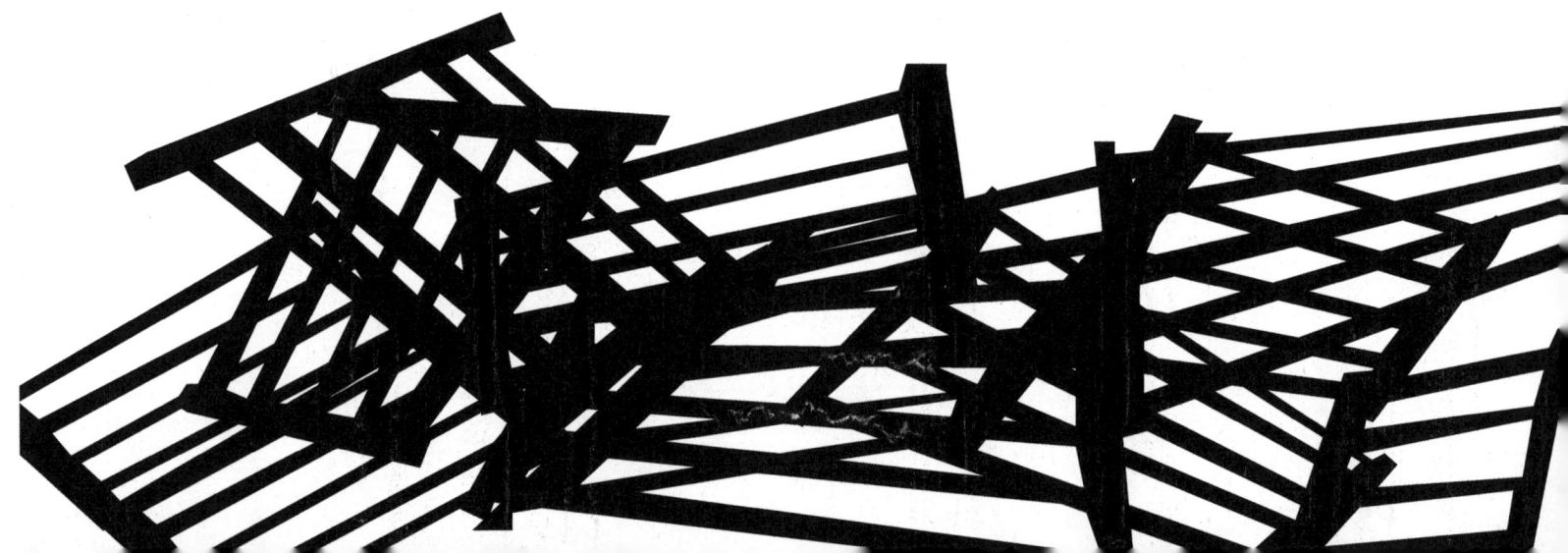

Milicent Wryght, malicious socialite,
ran out with a sinister grin,
and took the elevator to the roof in a rage—
there was only one way she could win.
She destroyed all the coops the pigeons were in,
and loosed the dazed birds up into the wind.

Milicent Wryght, self-serving socialite,
surely had no love inside,
and no sympathy for her hubby's grief
did she even attempt to supply.
He sat in somber silence and cried,
and all his fondness for Mili quickly died.

Milicent Wryght, Manhattan socialite,
to her total shock and dismay,
could barely believe her husband's decision
to walk out for good that day.
Even worse——the pigeons returned to stay
on her fancy terrace to coo, romp, and play.

Milicent Wryght, jilted socialite,
was now living her life on her own.
She stayed in her Manhattan penthouse,
with her wealth, but all alone.
She shunned society and remained at home,
except for her treks when she'd gripe and groan.

Milicent Wryght, spiteful socialite,
made her way down Park Avenue each day.
She snarled at people, puppies, and babes,
and kicked pigeons that got in her way,
With a venomous look that seemed to say,
"You horrible creatures—I'll make you pay!"

Milicent Wryght, evil-minded socialite,
disliked pigeons from head to toe.
Their cooing from the terrace drove her mad,
a reminder of the time years ago.
She saw them as the cause of all of her woes,
and one day decided they'd all have to go.

Milicent Wryght, shifty socialite,
gazed with hate at the birds through her window.
A plan for revenge filled her disdainful heart—
to dole out vile toxic edible blows
to the poor helpless pigeons that were under her nose,
with no thought of the adage, "One reaps what one sows."

Milicent Wryght, vindictive socialite,
baked some devilish dough that day.
With a dash of arsenic here and there,
honed the recipe for her cooing prey.
Silent and steady was her plan to slay
all the pigeons in a sure-fire culinary way.

Milicent Wryght, Manhattan socialite,
lured the pigeons to her terrace on high,
with sweet-smelling poisoned crumbs of bread,
while humming a lullaby,
and watched them one by one wail, then die,
crying, "Bye-bye birdies, good riddance, goodbye!"

Milicent Wryght, vengeful socialite,
swept the dead birds from the terrace with a broom.
They fell to the ground without too much sound,
once the deadly food sealed their doom.
With the sidewalk below as their uncovered tomb,
how she wished one would land on her former bridegroom.

Milicent Wryght, pernicious socialite,
waged for years her killing campaign,
along with her wroth walks down Park Avenue,
stomping through sunshine or rain.
Angry at life, bitter, scorned, and insane,
it seemed this was how she would always remain.

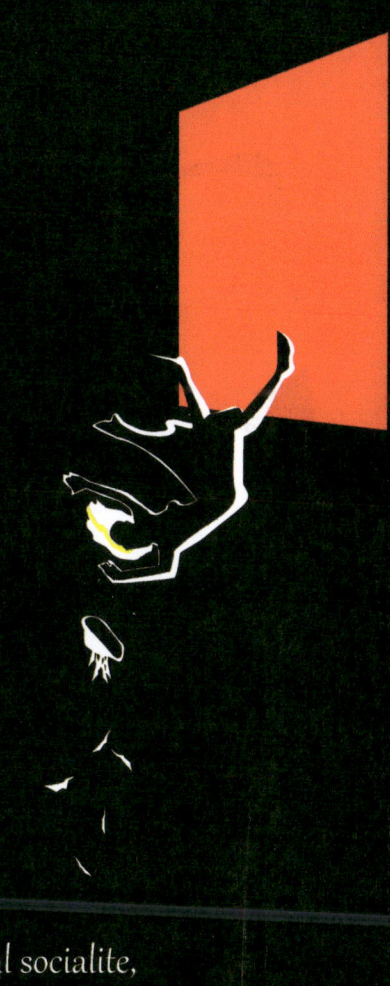

Milicent Wryght, lethal socialite,
headed out in an old feathered hat.
With a Cheshire Cat grin,
to the elevator she strolled,
distracted, counting birds she'd attacked.
When the door opened to a deep, empty shaft,
she plummeted down—
and splat! That was that!

Milicent Wryght, Manhattan socialite,
did indeed on that fateful day die.
The plumes on her hat were askew and awry—
if she'd been a bird, she'd have flown to the sky.
Some might have thought 'twas an eye for an eye,
an end fitting her deeds, no one could deny.

Milicent Wryght, Manhattan socialite,
lay dead on the dreary shaft floor.
Then, a curious noise could be heard from the place
where Mili breathed no more.
'Twas a bird's "midge-midge" chirp filled with profuse rancor—
a sound second-rate to her voice from before.

Milicent's soul was no longer hers—
from her dismal tomb it did fly.
Unaware she'd reincarnated into a bird,
she was squeaking the queer midge-midge cry.
From the corner of one of her black beady eyes,
caught a glimpse of herself in some glass
and thought, *Why?!*

Midge-midge, miserable Manhattan pigeon,
now condemned to a fate on a sill,
flew to the penthouse, put her beak on the glass—
her former life no longer hers to fulfill.
Curled up in the corner to avoid getting chills,
reflecting on her now fellow birds she had killed.

Midge-midge, pigeon with no pedigree,
to indulge a persistent need,
turned to crime picking pockets on the Big Apple streets,
executed with great skill and speed.
She flew off with baubles, bangles, and beads,
then pecked at stray crumbs and sometimes birdseed.

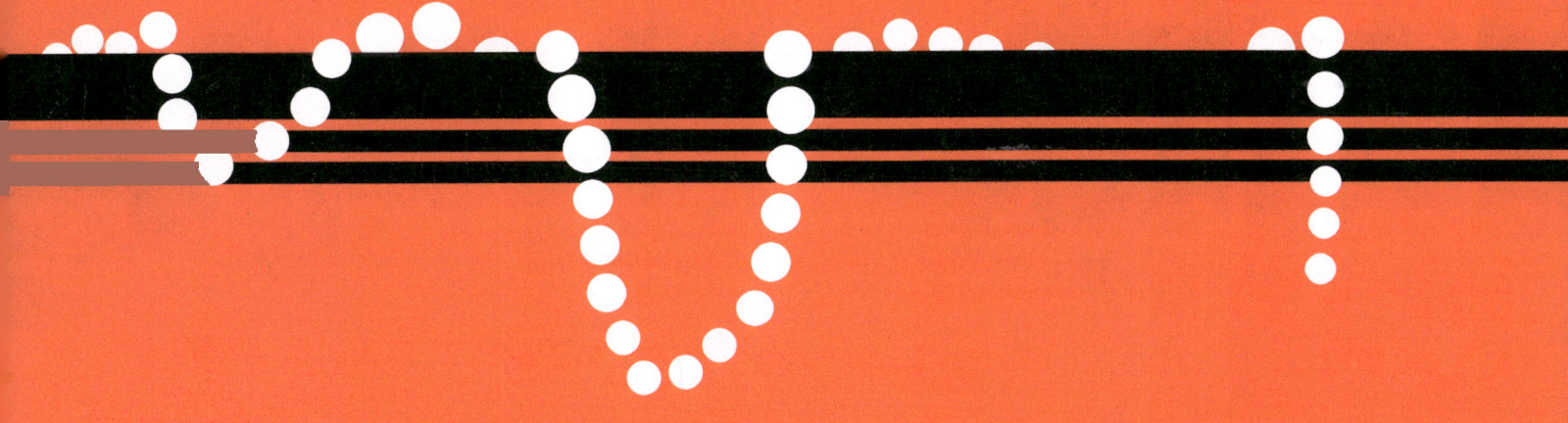

Midge-midge, petulant Park Avenue pigeon,
hoarded all her keen beak could steal.
Earrings, scarves, odd gloves, strings of pearls—
an attempt to appear more genteel.
In spite of her costumes du jour for appeal,
she would never escape her ill-fated ordeal.

Midge-midge, pensive Park Avenue pigeon,
knew Mili's jealousy drove her husband away,
and she'd kept her penthouse, furs, and jewels,
when he left 'cause of her bullying ways.
As though she'd shooed him with a broom's quick sway,
like his precious prized pigeons she had chosen to slay.

Midge-midge, pitiful Park Avenue pigeon,
one afternoon heard whispered sounds
coming from inside the lavish penthouse—
peeked in and was shocked when she found
a man and a woman moving furniture around,
then saw a strange face staring back with a frown.

Midge-midge, hoarding Park Avenue pigeon,
could see from the new tenant's face,
she viewed Midge-midge's cache of stolen loot
as quite slovenly and morally base.
The entire terrace ledge was a total disgrace,
only fit for a "rat with wings'" dwelling place.

After her survey of the cluttered ledge,
the gal fetched a broom and some feed.
Midge-midge, truly impenitent pigeon,
in a flash saw her past evil deeds.
"Oh, no!" Midge-midge screeched,
then made a faux plea,
fraught with fear she cried out,
"I'M SORRY! FORGIVE ME!"

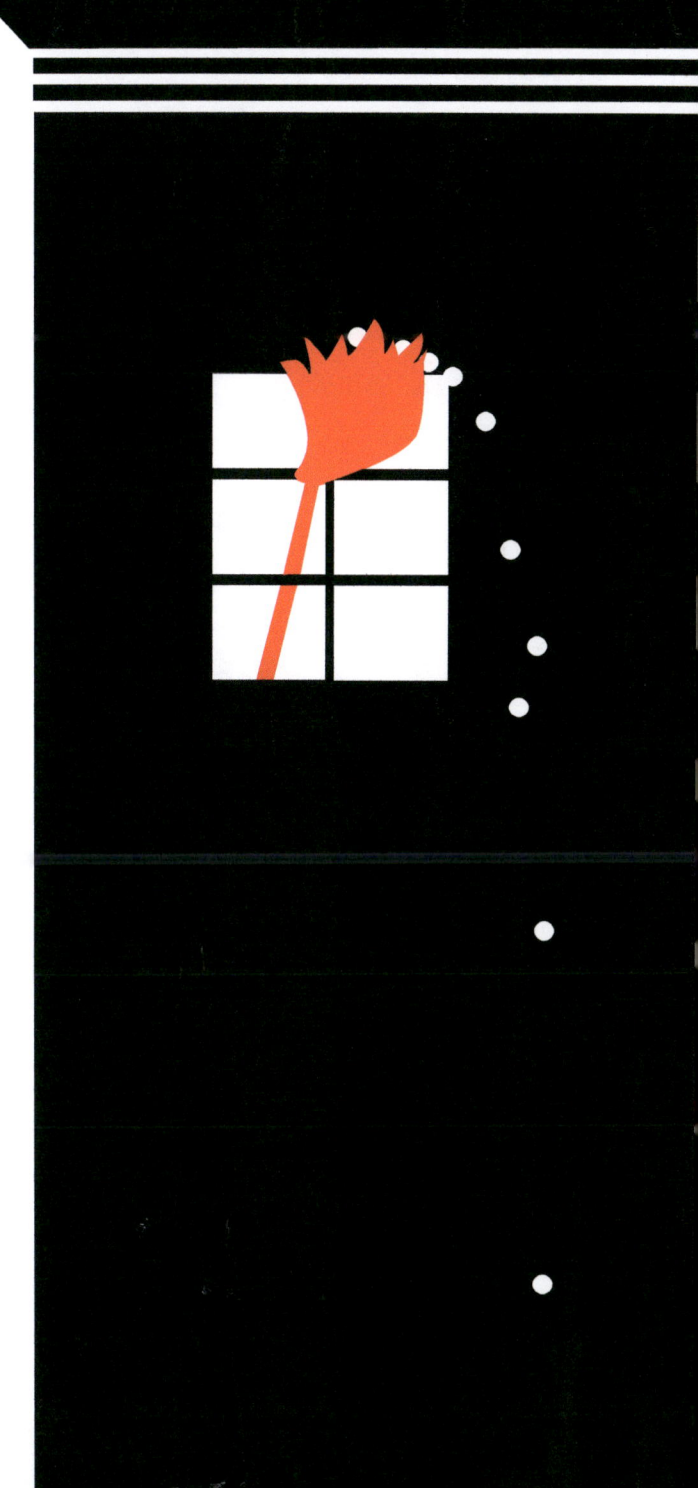

Midge-midge, evicted taciturn pigeon,
escaped the broom that day,
but her fate was sealed, no turning back—
evermore, a pigeon she'd stay.
From roof to ledge, she'd land and lay,
until the next broom shooed her away.

ABOUT THE AUTHOR

 Joanne de Simone is an author, dramatist, and film historian. Two of her seven plays, "The Suicide Angel," and "Earthmen," are currently in film pre-production, and several one-acts have been produced in NYC theatre festivals. Joanne's, "Judy's Dead," took first prize in the Writer's Digest 79th Annual Stage Play Competition. Ms. de Simone's full-length play, "Olivia's Roses," debuted at NYC's Thespis Theater Festival in September 2015. Her film review column appeared in the Fire Island News from 1998-2003 and returned for the 2015 season. Joanne's work has been published in various magazines, publications, and film journals. She has written a children's book, "The Metro Cats: Life in the Core of the Big Apple," and a young adult book, "The Peculiar Plight of Milicent Wryght," both urban tales set in Manhattan. Joanne is a member of the Dramatists Guild, the English Speaking Union, the Shakespeare Guild, the Episcopal Actors Guild, the Drama League, is a board member of the Veronica Moscoso Foundation, and serves as a judge for the Hudson River Classics Showcase Theater Playwriting Contest.

ABOUT THE ILLUSTRATOR

Annette Lee is currently a student at the School of Visual Arts in New York City, and is interning in the Design Department for Penguin Random House. She is an aspiring art director, majoring in both graphic design and advertisement. This is Annette's first book project, and she looks forward to doing cover designs and illustrations for many more books and novels in the future.

www.ingramcontent.com/pod-product-compliance
Lightning Source LLC
Chambersburg PA
CBHW041541240626
47164CB00002B/81